DRAGH'S DEMISE

ISAAC HILL

EE HILL PUBLISHING

DEDICATION

To Bruce, thank you.

CHAPTER ONE

D ragh wrenched his sword forward, the blade releasing from the head he'd cleaved as he rode by the foot soldier. He looked forward, gripping his horse's body with his legs. His shoulder twinged, but he gripped the sword harder, pushing it up ahead of him into a high guard.

The rush of the ride was on him. One hand on the reins, one on his sword. He had been trained for battle, with sword and horse, from the time he could sit atop the beasts.

Time seemed to stand still as he rode; no war cries, no screams of the wounded. There was only the wind, the creaking of the saddle, the smell of leather and horse sweat in his nose.

His thighs were on fire, his back ached from the riding they'd already done.

In war, pain was forgotten. Dragh was at home in battle. His eyes locked in on the enemy.

Men scrambled out of the way, as Dragh and the men of the Eighth thundered across the open plane. Dragh could feel Praetorian Donn beside him, a presence that was never far from his side. He'd grown up with Donn at his side, always watching, always guiding. Donn had given him his first sword, a practice shaft of wood, and promptly put him on his behind. His father and mother had been too busy running the Kingdom, too busy for their son. Landor had needs.

"Push right!" A shout came from the cavalrymen on his left.

Dragh was at the head of the Squad of Cavalry, the tip of the spear thrust into the village that had revolted under Landor's rule. They'd killed the officials that his father, the King, had sent to govern.

King Kallen of Landor would not abide by that.

The rebels had been in a loose formation when the full Eighth Legion had crested a rise on their march to quell the villages in the south. An open plain stretched out in front of them, trees hemming it in on three sides.

The rebels were caught out on the open plain, on foot.

Dragh grimaced as the commands were passed down. The squad of cavalry were to ride into the flank of the enemy infantry. It would be a slaughter.

He sliced through a man's neck; the spray of blood hit his face as he urged his horse on. The blood was hot and metallic on his tongue.

"Dragh!" Donn called out from behind him.

Dragh ducked, the instinct trained into him by the Praetorian that had followed him since birth.

The whistling of arrows flew over him as he pushed his face and body down into the saddle.

"They have archers!" Dragh shouted, knowing that his voice would not carry, that it would not save his fellow Landorians.

"ARHHH!" A guttural scream came from behind him a moment later.

"ARCHERS!" Dragh shouted, rising from his horse's back as the enemy fired another volley from the rear of their formation.

Fear gripped him, twisting a knot into his stomach. Arrows knew only fate. If it was his time, the gods would guide the arrow to his breast. There was nothing a cavalry man could do but ride hard, killing their way to the archers.

Dragh didn't look back, he and Donn were lethal. Instead, he swung his sword again, down and out. He'd been fighting for so long with Donn at his side that he knew he'd be there.

Ferras skidded on his back hooves and reared up, forcing Dragh to hold on tight with his thighs. His stallion reared and struck out with his hooves, crushing a man's skull in a sickening crack.

Then, the killing done, Ferras leapt forward.

Dragh pushed to the right still, following the commands from Primus. Ferras crossed in front of another man, following the push and pull of Dragh's legs as they rode across the battlefield. The rebel raised up his sword, his fiery eyes telling Dragh that he was a believer in his cause.

Dragh drove down his heavy sword from left to right, slamming into the rebel's blade and carrying through into his shoulder. Blood spurted from the wound, splashing Dragh and his horse's side as they rode past.

Ferras snorted. The smell of blood always excited the horse. A warhorse of the North. The Tribes stock was from the mother herd, only captured after it had spent years in the mountains, surviving wild on their own.

Dragh's blade slid from his hand, the slick blood weakening his grip. The blade had dug too deep to pull out easily, and Ferras was galloping too fast.

Dragh drew another blade from across his body, a shorter stabbing sword.

The men in front of him were beginning to thin now. Dragh knew that they'd made it through the brunt of the men of Baratan, having seen the loose formation from the top of the hill in the north before charging their flank.

The archers were next, always at the back of the lines, far from the realities of war.

He gripped his sword tighter, focusing on the bowmen as they dropped their bows and arrows, pulling what bladed weapons they had.

Blood pumped in his ears, the noise all-consuming, as he rode hard.

These cowardly bastards killed from afar. He was about to teach them what steel tasted of up close.

Archers' arrows struck like the hands of the gods.

Dragh would introduce them to the gods now.

"FOR LANDOR!" Dragh shouted, his sword slicing through an archer's neck as he and Ferras wheeled back into the fray.

The squad cut through the archers of Baratan like a spear through the rain. None could withstand the wall of horse flesh that Landor had commanded as they destroy the flanks of their enemy. They rode diagonally through, cutting them in half and scattering them in chaotic groups.

Dragh felt cooling wind on his face as he cut his way free of the men of Baratan, the open plain and forest the only things in his sight now.

He sucked in fresh air, his lungs suddenly starving for breath.

Nothing made Dragh feel as alive as battle.

The sun shone down, the air crisp and clean, a slight breeze coming off the Car Lauch Mountains to their west.

Dragh closed his eyes, letting the wind clean his soul as he rode.

He focused on his horse, the gait they rode in, two hooves down, two up, freedom in-between. In-between the strikes on the earth, he and Ferras were weightless. Free.

He breathed in through his nose, calming his mind and heart.

Ferras snorted, bringing him back.

"TURN!" The shout came from behind Dragh again.

Pine trees were quickly getting larger as Dragh and Ferras galloped across the plain. The cavalry of the Eighth Legion had made quick work of the enemy.

Dragh turned his steed, pulling back slowly on the reins in a lazy arc to slow Ferras. The screams of the wounded sliced through the air far from the battle.

The feeling, more than anything, told him he was not alone.

"Sloppy kill, Prince," Legate Donn said between deep breaths.

Dragh slowed Ferras, finishing his turn and waiting for the rest of the squad. His horse and Donn's were the fastest in the Eighth Legion.

"You're almost as out of shape as that old nag of yours, Donn," Dragh said, wiping blood from his face.

"Dare not to speak ill of Kalle, she has done nothing to you." Donn rubbed his old horse's neck.

Dragh scoffed. "It's unbecoming of a Praetorian to ride such a steed. What if I had needed your blade?"

"It's unbecoming of a Sunborn to drop their blade." Donn asked, producing Dragh's sword that he'd left in a man's body on the battlefield.

"How'd you-?" Dragh asked.

Donn shrugged. "They train us Praetorians. You don't keep that sword, these men of Baratan might make quick work of you."

Dragh watched the remaining cavalry finish their pass through the rebels.

"Must be half of their army dead now," Donn said.

"If you could call it an army, Donn. This was slaughter." Dragh bit his tongue, stopping from saying more.

"We are a weapon to be used, young Sunborn," Donn said.

Dragh nodded, catching his breath and patting his horse's neck.

Ferras neighed, throwing his head back.

"I know," Dragh whispered to him. "You want to run. You"ll have your chance again soon."

The cavalry of the Eighth finished their arc, all lining up around Dragh and Donn.

"Always the head of the pack Dragh!" Wents shouted, stopped just beside Dragh and Donn.

"You know how royalty likes to take the best for itself!" Rikos said from Wents' side.

Dragh laughed, his noble friends from birth giving their usual comments.

"Sunborn! What are you waiting for?" Primus Ues reigned in beside Dragh and Donn along with the rest riders of the Eighth. Their horses snorted as they caught their breath.

Dragh looked over at the Primus. His armor was clean and shiny, not stained, battered or tarnished by battle.

Dragh looked back to the killing fields they'd ridden through.

The sun rose above them in its morning ascent. The heat was rolling off it, warming the earth. A slight mist rose from the ground across the battlefield. If not for the wielding of death, the stain of killing, this place would be beautiful.

Dragh shook his head. Enough thoughts of beauty. He needed to focus.

"I asked you a question, Sunborn. We have orders to finish this." Primus Ues pushed his horse to Dragh's, forcing Ferras to push its rear against Ues's horse.

Ferras kicked up at Ues's horse, causing a stir of horses in the circle of cavalry.

The other beasts knew their better.

"Some respect, Ues," Donn growled.

Dragh put up a hand to stay Donn. The Praetorian was breathing hard through his nose. Dragh knew the signs that Donn was ready to strike out. His Praetorian, Legate Donn outranked the Primus Ues, who was only in command of a Squad.

In the army of Landor, Dragh and Donn held no real power. He was there to learn to be commanded. A leader was useless if he could not listen. Princes were sent to be taught. However infuriating the learning.

A horn sounded in the distance, a twin picking up the call.

The sound made it to the cavalry, a signal from the General. It echoed across the plains, a sharp sound above the screams and chaos that Ues' squad had sowed.

Ues wrinkled his nose. his slight face giving the look of a petulant child. "We go back into the blood, men!"

"If we ride through the Baratans's from the rear, we will kill our own infantry squads coming from the north." Dragh gave the Primus a look of disbelief.

Ues shook his head. "You have NO authority here, boy! You are in this squad, and you will listen to me."

"Going through will put our own men at risk, Ues. Think man, think!" Dragh urged the Primus of the Cavalry, his voice low enough that it would not travel to the rest of the men.

Ues spit on the ground between them. "ORDERS, SUNBORN!" Ues waved his clean sword in the air, a signal to the rest of the men to move.

Donn and his horse, Kalle, bristled.

Ues turned, his eyes alight with anger. "Don't even think about it, Praetorian. You are here for Dragh, but that won't stop me from hanging you for insubordination."

Donn looked back to Dragh, then to Ues.

Dragh clenched his jaw, stopping himself from shouting down his commanding officer. He knew that Ues was in command, but he couldn't believe the Primus would put the infantry of the Eighth at risk to follow the General's orders blindly.

Bloodlust had taken over his reasoning.

Dragh clenched his jaw. "The infantry—"

Ues cut Dragh off. "The General gave orders to us, Sunborn. We ride!"

Ues put his sword up, whirling it around. And then, bringing it down, he pointed forward, across the field of battle they'd just ridden through.

Ues and the men of the Eighth's cavalry stormed forward, horses braying, men urging their mounts to follow their Primus.

Dust swirled up from under horses' hooves.

Dragh nodded to Wents and his nobles who followed after Ues.

Dragh gripped his sword, his knuckles turning white. He blinked through the dust cloud. He knew his father had sent him here to learn. He could not understand why the King of Landor would suffer such fools in his army. He wanted to shout at Ues, to rage against the stupidity.

"Ues is going to get men of the infantry killed, charging from the rear of the Barnatans."

Donn nodded to Dragh. "We are here to fight." Donn reached out, leaning in his saddle and gripped Dragh's shoulder. "We Serve."

"I'm a Sunborn," Dragh said, spitting on the ground.

Donn had been his shadow for all of Dragh's life, as far back as he could remember. An ever-present force of nature. They'd spent so long together, they could feel each other's currents. The deep ones that moved within a man's heart.

Donn laughed. "What is the lesson, boy?"

Dragh snorted. He looked Donn over. The man had also been sprayed with blood, his armor under the gore clean, a polish on the metal breastplate. There was some grey in his beard, but his eyes were alive, keen and focused.

Dragh could see the cavalry charging through the rear of the men of Baratan. It was like watching a bounder roll down a mountain. Their momentum was not altered by the ragtag army of villagers.

Ues would be through in moments, and into the Eighth infantry.

Dragh shook his head. "The lesson is that Primus is a fool."

Donn chuckled and shook his head.

"The lesson is that Generals and Kings have plans."

Dragh bit back a retort. "And that we must follow this fool. Come."

Dragh knew that men like Ues did not forget. There was no give in his capacity for spite.

Dragh drove his heels into Ferras's side, knowing that Ferras was waiting for his signal to run, knowing that Donn would follow.

CHAPTER TWO

"He asks what I was thinking? What was his *Legate* thinking? He should have put that snake's feet to the fire, not mine," Dragh almost shouted.

Donn grunted as they led their horses down the main thoroughfare of the camp the Eighth had set up.

The open air camp was General Serras's idea; it sat just north of the center of Baratan, the rebels' home base. They'd set the camp up in rows, four on each side of a main thoroughfare. The command tent in the middle, facing Baratan's settlement.

Tents were flapping in the breeze, the sound of a war camp all around them. Men shouted, laughed and argued. The blacksmith's anvil rang, cooks spits turned, water from wash basins sloshed and spilled to the ground.

Dragh could smell the sweet pine needles in the smoke of the fires. The forests were softwood in the southlands.

The village of Baratan was in an area south of Landor, and north of the Junis River. All bordered by the spine of the Car Lauch mountains that ran from north to south, hemming them in.

The city of Landor was the capital of his father's nation of the same name. It was made up of different provinces that owed his father, and the Sunborns, their allegiance. This small village was inside his father's province.

And so the duty of doling out the King's justice fell to the Landorian Army. The Eighth Legion.

"You know that you are a target. He has to let his men know that he is in charge, not the Sunborn—what did he call you?"

Dragh grimaced. "Pup,"

"Yes. The Sunborn pup," Donn chuckled.

"I thought you were supposed to defend me; what would my father think of this?" Dragh raised an eyebrow at Donn.

Donn nodded along. "He'd think, there is the trusted Legate Donn, old and wise in the ways of the world, helping the young *pup* learn the old ways."

Dragh and Donn continued to walk their horses through camp, leading them to the picket line on the far side of the tents.

"Agh. We've been here for days now. Why did the General wait so long to address his men?"

Dragh knew that his father wanted them to bow. He sent out a Legion to teach them a lesson.

Donn's face grew dark. "I know not the plans of the King. I am a simple Praetorian. Nothing more." Donn paused and looked around as they walked. "I hear that he was sending a message to the Baratans."

"What message?" Dragh asked, catching the dark look on Donn's face.

Donn pursed his lips and stopped amid the sea of tents. He lowered his voice. "He sent back the bodies of the slain soldiers." Donn closed his eyes, shaking his head. "He sent them in pieces."

"Zufier above," Dragh whispered back.

Donn kept walking. Kalle bent down and nudged the grain sack at his side.

Ferras nickered and leaned into Dragh, almost pushing him over.

"What do you think they will do? Sue for peace?" Dragh asked.

Donn didn't stop this time; he kept walking. He said it so quickly, so low, that Dragh had to strain to hear it.

"The question is, will the General accept peace?"

Dragh thought on that. Knowing his father's orders were brutal, horrible, he wondered at what General Serras would do.

They made it to the rear of the camp, a picket line set up north of camp to allow the horses a little freedom.

They brushed down their horses and slipped grain sacks over their ears.

Dragh thought on Donn's comment. Why wouldn't the General accept peace? If he was sent here to subdue the village of Baratan, then wouldn't that achieve his mission? He wondered what his father had commanded of his General.

—---

"It's all women and children, not a single man out there," Harvel said to the men around the fire.

The crackling of the wet wood in their fire pit and the shooting coals from the pockets of wet were their entertainment for the night. Darkness settled around them, after they'd eaten their supper, a cold wind along with it.

Donn leaned down, passing Dragh a plate of food. Dragh nodded his thanks to Donn.

The Praetorian said nothing, sitting across from Dragh.

Dragh peered out into the dark. Their tent was in the middle of the camp, close to the command tent of General Serras. The moon gave just enough light that Dragh could see across to the small village of Baratan beyond them, its torches bright around the houses and huts.

No men of war had come out from the village when they'd marched to its very doorstep. Dragh knew that if any were left alive, they would have. Men and women of Landor were proud people. He couldn't help but think of the generation of men and boys that they'd killed in their skirmish. Brothers and sons, husbands and fathers.

All of them dead. For what?

"They hardly have defenses. Why don't we just go in there and take the place?" Rikos asked.

Dragh sighed.

"Oh, enlighten us, great Sunborn," Wents gave a mock bow from his seat across from Dragh.

Rikos, Wens and Garin were all in the Cavalry Squads of the Eighth Legion, in the same squad as Dragh, under Primus. They were all nobles, families with names in Landor. All of them built for combat: broad shoulders, tall, good teeth and hair. All of them had the gait of a cavalry man, strength in their legs from years in the saddles.

The common man or woman in Landor couldn't afford such leisure time on a horse. Only the rich could.

"You never go out and stab your neighbour when he pisses you off. You'll end up with a knife in your guts when you go to sleep." Harvel spit into the fire and wiped his mouth with his sleeve.

Harvel was an archer from the Eighth. Dragh didn't know what squad he belonged to. He appeared one night. Sauntered up to their fire and didn't seem to leave. When they sat down, he would appear.

"He's right. If they destroy this village, it will only inspire others to revolt," Dragh agreed.

At first Dragh had been concerned that Harvel was a spy for the General or another Legate, but Donn checked around. He was from the slums outside Landor. He was a pretty man, his hair always kempt. His shoulders broader than all of them, his only odd feature was a crooked nose that had been broken and never reset.

"A Kings justice is always swift." Harvel said lowly.

Dragh looked over at the archer, watching the man as he tore small pieces off his loaf of bread. His hands were gloved, the dark leather protecting his hands when he pulled at his bow string.

"What does little Harv know of the justice of kings?" Wents made fun of the archer, giving an over the top flourish of his hand.

Harvel chuckled darkly. "You all think you know what this is like? What it is like for the people over there?" Harvel jutted his chin towards Baratan.

"Don't tell me that you think you do, that you know of the strife they endure. Save me your pity story." Rikos rolled his eyes.

Dragh kept his mouth shut, knowing that whatever Harvel was about to share was at his fathers commands. Whatever this man had endured.

Rikos and Wents went on, making fun of the archer.

Dragh watched, the archer's stare concentrated on the fire.

Harvel pulled at his gloved hands, pulling one finger at the time until the glove slipped off his right hand. Then his left.

Rikos and Wents both stopped talking.

"Pit." Garin said.

Harvel put both of his hands up, splaying the fingers.

Dragh looked at the mans hands, rough and flat at the tips from hard use all of his life. He almost missed the scars, pocked and white covering all of the back of the archers hands.

Harvel looked at his hands, his eyes still distant. "You see, where I am from, crime is not necessary for punishment. I crossed the wrong man once. When I was very young. I lied to a guard at the market. Told him a little lie about another boy he'd seen stealing. Sent him in the wrong direction."

Harvel laughed.

"The man caught up with me. And he introduced me to fire. Told me that he'd teach me that all actions have consequences. That I'd cost him a bounty for a thief. And he'd take the cost out on my flesh."

All were silent around the fire.

Harvel pulled his gloves back on.

Dragh fought back tears for his friend. The cruelty of the story cutting him to the core.

"And look at you now, sitting round the fire, a loaf of bread for the poor in your hand," Rikos mocked.

Harvel gave Rikos a look. "You lot are just pissed off that we are equals now in this Pit."

Rikos laughed and then nodded.

The tension was broken now, the group of men back in good spirits after the dark confession.

"We all die the same when we get poked in the guts," Garin muttered.

Dragh felt sick, his stomach turning with the knowledge of what had been done to Harvel.

A Kings Justice.

There was silence for a time. Smoke wafted around them, the wind pushing it backward and forward.

Dragh looked back across the void between the camp and Baratan. He couldn't see the place now that the last light of the day had died, but he knew it was out there in the darkness to the south. They'd chosen not to light watch fires. They likely didn't have the defenders to man the walls.

He wondered at how the villagers must feel, looking at this Legion come to bring them to heel. From their perspective, it was lights, fires and shouting from the Legion' drunk soldiers. Thousands of men of Landor. All here for them. To bring order. All because they didn't like the taxes that his father had set on them.

How would he feel after an army had killed most of his kin able to fight? Wiped them out in one battle?

"An entire Legion sent here for one little village," Dragh mused.

"I hear that there is no fight left in these people." Rikos said.

"So? The king will do what he must here."

"The King has to show that he is lenient, that he can bring these people back into the fold. It's not like they attacked Landor," Harvel said.

"It seems the General wants to burn this place to the ground, from what I hear," Wents commented.

"What did they do?" Rikos asked.

Harvel looked at Rikos. "They refused to pay the king's taxes."

"The sword is the answer if your only question is what do we slice with."

The darkness of the night swallowed up each man's thoughts, time stretched out as Dragh felt his own fingers flex for his swords handle. He was that blade for his father's taxes.

"Zufier above," Rikos said.

Dragh said nothing, knowing that his father had ordered this. That there was no defense to what the king would do to keep order. He wondered if it was worth it, the killing that kept the kingdom.

Chapter Three

They were getting closer. Dragh could feel it. He could see the enemy.

Dragh gripped the saddle with his thighs, the ache in his back the price of speed.

His heart raced, his thrill of the hunt on him.

"Sunborn!" Primus Ues shouted as Dragh passed him.

Dragh smirked, his eyes never breaking the concentration on his prey.

Two men became clearer in the cloud of dust in front of Dragh. He squinted his eyes. He hated this part. The dust in his face, breathing it into his lungs. He wheezed but pushed on. The grit was almost too much to bear. But he needed this victory.

This army did not care that he was a Sunborn. In the Eighth, he had to prove his worth every day. To the men beside him, to his brothers in arms.

His father had told him to prove his worth. Prove he was more than just a name.

They were descending into a gully; Dragh recognized the hills gaining rise on either side of he and Ferras.

He passed another of the squad, the man cursing aloud as he did.

The enemies' horses were narrow and fast. He smiled. Ferras could out-run them all.

Dragh set his eyes on the leader of the pair. He had to finish this. One was not enough. The Eighth did not want a lone scout out in the wilderness to report on their strength, their movements. It was poison to any army.

Dragh knew that he and Donn would be the only two able to catch these men, the gap between them all growing larger and larger.

Dragh looked back, seeing Donn was too far behind him to catch up, hemmed in by the other cavalry. Donn nodded to Dragh, a knowing look.

"FERRAS! SINOVIS!" Dragh called out the name of the lost tribe, the Sinovi. Men of the mountains, guardians of the last emperor.

Ferras, his heart and lungs already pumping, threw his legs forward with reckless speed, a speed that only a pureblood could attain, a speed that made his line invaluable to the Sunborn family. The speed ensured that Ferras would never be gelded, that his bloodline would continue for generations.

Dragh held on with his legs, his hands soft on the rein. He transferred the rein to one hand and drew his sword between strides.

He sat high atop Ferras, moving as one with his mount.

Dragh could hear shouts in the distance, behind him, but he ignored them. The heat from the mid-day sun beat down on his face, making him squint in the dust and glare.

He was at the flank on the right of the first animals, the hills hemming them in.

Dragh could feel excitement building in his breast. He would stop these men, capture them or kill them. He'd trained for this his whole life.

The first of the pair, face wrapped in cloth, looked back at him, eyes wide. The enemies horses shouldn't have been able to out pace Ferras, especially after a gallop through the woods.

Dragh knew these must be men of Baratan, or their ilk. He silently thanked Ferras for his speed. He'd been prodigious in this chase. They were now at the rear of the second horse of the fleeing pair.

Dragh threw back his sword and brought it down on the man's leg from behind, ducking a wild swing from the fleeing man's sword.

The front hand's length of the blade cut into the man's leg.

The man screamed, dropping his sword.

Dragh kept moving, knowing he'd slowed the injured rider enough for the men of the Eighth to catch him.

The front man had thrown his garb from his face and was glaring back in glances at Dragh.

They were deep in the valley now, it's natural walls closing in on them.

Dragh could feel Ferras starting to slow, his stamina only able to last so long. He'd pushed his horse hard. He had only moments left at this breakneck speed.

Dragh crossed from the right to the left of the horse in front of him, switching his rein and his sword so that he didn't have to fight across his body.

His tutors had made sure he could fight with both hands.

His enemy hadn't changed hand, his sword in his left, opposite now of Dragh and his mount.

The man's neck and face-wrap worked loose, fluttering behind him in the wind. His eyes alight with hate. They locked eyes for a moment. The moment before battle passed like the falling water drop, collecting until it reached that critical weight, then dropping violently.

Dragh blocked the blow from below without conscious thought, the movement trained into him by years of practice.

The second strike from down low took Dragh by surprise. He'd trained his whole life for war. There were very few who could strike so quickly, across the body. How had this man been able to do that?

The men and women of Baratan were simple villagers. Farmers and weavers. Fishermen. Dragh was a highly trained solider. A sword in hand since he was old enough to hold a wooden blade. How the Pit had this man done that?

There was something more than Baratan attempting to overthrow the rule of Landor at play here. It was more than farmers and fishermen aligned against them.

Dragh redoubled his efforts and threw his own strike, meeting steel.

A crosscut, on horseback, blocked from low to up high across the body.

Dragh blocked again.

Dragh knew he was matched in swordwork. This man was a master with the blade.

He pushed Ferras with his outside knee. Ferras responded, driving the other horse and rider towards the rise in land.

It was lightly forested here, almost an open plain.

Dragh and the rider exchanged more blows, each of them, back and forth, met with its sister sword. His arm began to tire, his shoulders burning with effort, his legs numbing.

Dragh needed to stop this horseman, to keep him alive.

He had questions for this man. The Eighth needed to know what they were facing.

Dragh glanced forward, trusting his horse, but needing to know if there was anything ahead he could use to his advantage.

The valley itself ended, a wide-open space ahead of it.

In these foothills of the Car Lauch, you needed to be careful. Sudden drops were gullies, an invitation for the careless rider to die. If he kept pushing this enemy, he could ensure that there was nowhere to go. The hills on either side were too high and steep for horses. Even Ferras wouldn't make it up the sides.

Dragh kept the rider hemmed in, hoping that he'd stop, or push his horse hard enough not to be able to stop.

Dragh's left shoulder felt the sting of the cut from the enemies blade.

All men of the army knew that with the shallow ones, you felt everything. The deep ones where you felt nothing would kill you.

He felt the wet tell tale of blood on his hand as he pushed Ferras harder. As he lifted his blade, he was side swiped by a branch of a tree. The branch his arm and with the blood slicked grip he dropped his sword.

Dragh pulled his short sword from his belt, just in time to block a blow to the guts.

The man shouted in a language Dragh didn't understand. The man's eyes were alight with anger.

Dragh glanced forward, the void at the end of the valley growing even closer.

Dragh knew he had to finish this. His eyes were watering from the speed of the ride, his back ached, his wound on his shoulder was bleeding. He was just able to hang on to Ferras.

Dragh pushed the man and horse into the almost sheer wall with Ferras. Bracing for the impact, he fought the urge to close his eyes just before he hit the other horse. He felt the lurch of Ferras responding to his push inward.

He lost the battle, his eyes snapping shut within moments of the collision.

Branches and scrub smacked his face. The impact numbed his mouth and cheek.

Dragh opened his eyes, the pain searing and hot. His face was a hand from the sheer face of the hill. He righted himself atop Ferras by throwing himself the other way as he hung almost out of the saddle.

He looked around in confusion, pulling back on the rein to slow Ferras.

The man he'd been chasing, the foreigner with fire in his eyes, was mounting the wall of the valley with his horse.

Dragh's mouth fell open. It should have been impossible.

Dragh let Ferras cool, walking him out as the rest of the squad caught up to them. Donn's horse was first to meet them, Praetorian stock akin to the Sunborn herd. Then his noble friends, Rikos, Wents and Garin.

Ues followed, almost at the back of the squad.

"What the Pit did you let that man get away for?" Ues asked, sneering at Dragh.

Dragh swallowed his pride. "He matched my every stride, by every blow with a sword. I did what I could, Ferras too."

The cavalrymen were now arrayed in a circle, except for those assigned to guard duty. They were out, watching the surrounding valley.

Dragh looked up, shaking his head in disbelief. He couldn't see a sign of the man that had escaped him. The pair had gone up and over the walls and was out of his grasp.

What kind of animal and rider could have done that?

"They must be from the Plains. The far Wast. None in Landor could match Ferras."

Ues rolled his eyes. "I've heard enough about your mixed breed rat that you ride on. Sunborn or not, you'll answer for letting an enemy of the crown get away."

"He didn't let them get away. They climbed the side of a wall, Ues," Donn spoke up for Dragh.

For a moment, there was more tension between Ues and Donn. Horses and men alike felt the ripple of promised violence between them.

Ues turned his horse and broke rank.

The men that followed for following's sake, followed Ues.

Some dipped their heads at Dragh, knowing he'd done what he could.

Legate Donn moved beside Dragh.

The retreating Primus infuriated Dragh. How could he think that Dragh had done this? That the escaping man was his fault?

"Did you drop this again?" Legate Donn held up Dragh's sword.

Dragh grunted his thanks.

Donn gripped Dragh's shoulder. "Let's get that wound bound."

Dragh looked back at his shoulder, the wound forgotten in his anger for Ues. "I have to speak to that other horseman. They were not from Baratan, Donn. Something is going on here."

Donn nodded. "They outmatched Ferras. I've not seen such skill outside of the deserts of the Horde to the west."

"Did they capture the other man?" Dragh asked.

"Let us see what he can tell us." Donn flicked his rein, prompting his horse to move on.

Dragh clucked at Ferras, who'd by now recovered from their hard ride.

Dragh and his nobels moved as a pack. They followed the first group who had gone with Ues without comment.

Some loyalties were bigger than the chain of command. Some were to justice, to right and wrong.

Some were to the bloodline. Forever.

They heard the other group as they approached, the dust floating off the trail, puffs of it telling them they were not far behind.

Shouts were all around as Dragh and his men made it back along the trail to the prisoner.

Dragh slid off his horse and handed it to Wents, who'd stayed mounted.

They shared a nod.

He pushed forward into a horseshoe crowd to the center of the gathered men.

"String him up!" Ues shouted.

They'd surrounded the largest tree in the Valley in sight.

One of the scouts had bound the shrouded man's hands, an open wound on his leg still bleeding from where Dragh had struck him.

The man was weathered from days in the sun. He had a bloody nose and mouth. His right eye was swollen shut. The one that was open was searching the crowd, a scowl on his face.

The Eighth's scout pushed him forward, onto his knees in front of the crowd.

Ues pranced in front of the men, back and forth. He held up his sword, pointing to the tree. "Let us see him swing!"

Dragh was now in the inner circle, closing in on Ues.

A rope was thrown by one of the cavalrymen.

A noose swung in the heat of the day, its form injecting fear into the look of the wounded man.

"Stop this, he's not Baratan!" Dragh shouted at Ues, stepping forward to his Primus.

Ues jeered again. "General says no prisoners! Let's show this lot what we do to traitors of Landor!"

Dragh buried his anger. Ues was ignoring him.

The crowd cheered at the words.

Dragh looked around. The men had blood lust on their mind. Their cheers were those of a drunken rabble.

"Ues! Stop this! We need to know who he is, who he's with!" Dragh shouted, making it to Ues as the little man nodded to the cheering men of the squad.

Ues sneered at Dragh, his eyes narrowing. "Hang HIM!"

"ENOUGH!" Dragh bellowed, meeting Ues' glare.

"Orders, boy," Ues spit out, a challenge in the words.

Dragh gripped his sword, fighting the urge to back his words up with steel. "This is murder."

"What did you say *boy?*" Ues said, louder this time.

The men of the Eighth were quiet.

Dragh took half a step, his sword sliding out of the scabbard.

A hand settled on Dragh's shoulder, a hand he'd felt many times in his life.

Dragh knew what Legate Donn would say.

Dragh shook his head and turned. Brushing off Donn's hand on his shoulder. Walking past his nobles that had come with him.

None of them had backed Dragh in words or actions. None would challenge the authority of the General and Primus Ues.

CHAPTER FOUR

"Here's your chance boy. Show us what the Sunborn can do."

The challenge hung in the air spoken like a threat by the General.

Donn sucked in air at it.

Dragh felt his blood boil, heat in his face. "The scout's report was clear. There's naught but women and children here."

"They are hiding the martial men of the village! They cannot see what is hidden within." Ues repeated the line that many in the command tent had. Hanging onto it like the lip of a cliff they might fall off.

Dragh knew it was the justification of weak men. Men with blood lust. He looked around at the men in the tent: Legates, Primus's and the General of the Eighth, General Seras; a tall man with a hawkish face.

The tent was furnished in decadence. The men of the army stood, but the tent had intricately carved tables, chairs, tables; rugs and furs; pitchers of wine and ale, water; and of course a roast cooking over the fire pit.

The sweet smell of roasting meat gave the distasteful orders a sweet smell, making Dragh sick to his stomach.

"You would kill a thousand innocents?" Dragh shot back, repeating the intelligence gathered by the Eight's own advanced scouts over the week.

"The KING commands us. We will crush this rebellion," the General said softly.

Dragh breathed in through his nose, out through his mouth. Donn was behind him. Forbidden to speak in the tent by the General himself, except to protect Dragh, his charge.

Dragh was only there to learn, outranked in the army by all present.

"You have no proof, no evidence. That fool killed the only person we could have questioned!" Dragh pointed to Ues.

"As I reported, sir, the man had no information for us. He was dispatched as commanded," Ues said.

"Lies," Dragh growled at his Primus. "The men we chased had better horses than even me. They traversed the side of a bloody mountain at a gallop."

This was met by snorts, cut short by a mean look from the General to his gathered command.

Dragh pulled at his breath, trying to calm himself. He couldn't believe that these men would be so easily led into stupidity. So willingly led to the murder of innocent men and women.

"They escaped because Dragh let the lone rider go," Ues said.

"And they looked to be men of the desert, of the Horde, not like the men of Baratan. Someone else is helping these rebels!" Dragh protested.

The General looked to Legate Qural, Ues' superior.

"Sir, the men were described by the rest of Ues's squad as Baratans. We have no reason to believe that anyone else is helping the Baratans," Qural said.

Dragh looked to the Legate in disbelief. "They were of the desert. The only peoples like that are the Horde!"

The General shook his head and walked over to Dragh slowly.

"Sunborn, you are here to learn, not to disrupt this Legions business. You will execute this mission. That is an order from your General."

Dragh looked back at the General, disbelief on his face. "I will not kill innocents. My father would never give such a command."

General Seras smiled.

Dragh felt his stomach drop. His guts turn.

He'd been caught in a trap. One that the General, that even Ues had sprung on him.

"Your father commanded me to quell Baratan by any means necessary," The General looked around his command tent. "We, the loyal subjects to Kallen Sunborn, will follow those orders. It is after all, the way a Kingdom is kept, *boy.*"

Everyone was quiet, still.

The only sound was the roast dripping fat into the fire as it turned over, the creaking of turning gears of the spit.

"If killing hundreds of innocents, a thousand, is the way a Kingdom is kept, I'd rather die than take the crown."

Dragh locked eyes with the General. He was here to serve, but he would not betray his own honor.

Seras smiled. "Legate Donn. You know the cost of disobeying a direct order, don't you? The King wills it, and the son refuses,"

Donn stepped forward "You cannot. You will not."

General Seras mocked the statement, putting his hand on his breast.

There was uneasy laughter from around the tent. The lackeys of Seras following their man's lead.

Dragh felt control slipping away from him. He was a Prince, a Sunborn. He was in line for the throne. How could a General do this to him? Yet, it was so. All Sunborns were sent to the army, to learn, to serve the machines of death at their command when they ascended to the throne.

A look of satisfaction passed over Serras's face.

"Ues, you and your men will escort Dragh AND Donn to their quarters. They are under arrest by my command," the General smiled, his face contorting into an ugly, menacing thing.

Dragh's mouth fell open.

The sea of red and gold, usually a comfort, were now walls, closing in on him.

Dragh was still when they came for him, moving with them in disbelief that they were taking him away. That they were laying their hands on him.

For the first time in his life, he didn't say a word.

CHAPTER FIVE

"**M**ake sure they do not leave this tent." Ues barked behind Dragh and Donn.

Dragh wrenched his shoulder free of the guard who'd escorted him from the General's war party.

They were positioned outside of Donn and Dragh's tent, inside the row of tents of the Eighth.

Ues shook his head and turned on his heel, walking away.

Ues had four men, two for Donn and two for Dragh.

"Go back to your master, *dog*," Dragh spit at Ues's turned back.

Ues turned, his face red.

Dragh spit on the ground, a halfhearted thing that landed just in front of his own feet.

One of the soldiers guarding them pushed Dragh forward.

Dragh stumbled, and then righted himself. He wouldn't give the guard the satisfaction of a response.

"You touch him like that again, and I will kill you all," Donn said quietly.

Ues glared at Donn as the four guards looked to him and then back to Donn.

Dragh let them soak in fear. He could feel it rolling off of them, the way that smoke issues from a wet fire, low and steady, suffocating.

Donn was feared in the Eighth.

The king of Landor had sent his only son to war. He had sent him with a hound from the Pit in tow to protect him.

Ues took two slow steps toward Dragh.

"Dog, eh? You prance about this camp with your little friends. Your *nobles*. While the rest of us soldiers do the real work of this army. The army your father sent on this mission."

Dragh narrowed his eyes at Ues, biting his tongue.

Ues scoffed, shaking his head at Dragh. "You see. Right there. You want so badly to tell me I'm wrong, how smart you are. How I'm a dog. But guess what, Dragh? I am a soldier. I follow orders. Dog? At least I'm not a wild mutt who won't do what he's told. Because some day, that dog gets put down."

"Enough, Ues." Donn said from behind Dragh.

Ues nodded. "You call me a dog, but I do my job. Enough is when I say it is, Praetorian."

Dragh worked his jaw, keeping his mouth shut.

Ues nodded to the nervous guards beside Dragh.

"Take these men out of here; they are confined to this tent on orders of the General."

Dragh shook his head at Donn, seeing the man's face go blank.

Dragh knew that Donn was clearing his mind, preparing for battle.

Donn gave a short nod back.

—---

Dragh sat on a bench in his tent, head in his hands. He needed at his temples, playing back the last two weeks.

"They cannot have been of Baratan. Something else is going on here Donn."

Donn grunted in response.

The tent they shared was large enough for them to walk a few paces, and then to turn. But only one of them at a time.

"You're making me dizzy. Sit," Dragh groaned at Donn who paced the tent.

Donn stopped, looking at Dragh. "Your father will have Serras's head."

Dragh barked a laugh. "I suspect the King will commend the General for teaching his petulant son a lesson."

Donn blew out a breath through his nose. "We need to leave. We need to get back to Landor. This is an insult to the crown."

Dragh shook his head. "We must play the hand, Donn. We need to stop him from killing those people. Something else is going on here.

Something more sinister than Baratan throwing out the Landorian tax collectors."

"You think another nation is playing the puppeteer?"

Dragh pursed his lips. "Or the Council."

Silence stretched out, filling up the tent.

Donn began to pace again.

"Guard!" Dragh shouted, his head hung in his hands. His elbows braced on his knees.

A young man threw open the tent flap and came into the tent.

Dragh looked up and then put his head back in his hands.

The young man was average height, slightly larger build than Rikos, with a little scruff on his face. His eyes had been hardened when Dragh had glanced up.

"What's your name?" Dragh asked.

Dragh looked back up at the boy. He looked uncomfortable now, his back rigid, his eyes looking between Donn and Dragh. He looked uncertain, the hardened look of a soldier replaced by the confused look of a boy.

Dragh knew from his father, to ask questions first was to put your enemy off guard. They always expected force from a man in power.

"You know who I am?" Dragh asked.

"Ye-yes sir." The young man stood a little straighter.

"Your Highness," Donn whispered.

The boy looked over at the Praetorian, and then back to Dragh.

"Yes, your Highness."

Sweat beaded on the boy's forehead; the morning heat had infiltrated the tent that Donn shared with Dragh. Not the striking heat of the day, but the stifling heat of the humid mornings.

"What is your name?" Dragh asked, softer this time.

The boy raised his hand to salute, then thought better of it. "Name's Asof, sire."

Dragh stood, and took a step to the boy, closing the distance easily to stand in front of him. "You can drop the sire crap. You know who I am, you know who he is. It's Dragh, nothing more in this army."

The boy looked to Donn and then back to Dragh. "Yes, your highness,"

Dragh shook his head.

Donn had this effect on people. He was slim but built like a swordsman. His skill with the blade far surpassed anyone Dragh had met.

"You're going to let us out of here. We have business to attend to," Donn said from across the small tent.

Dragh looked to the tent walls; the sound of men and horses moving in force made its way through the thin white fabric of the tent walls.

The young Landorian, Asof, looked down, his eyes scanning empty scabbards of both Dragh and Donn before answering. He took a deep breath and looked back up with determination.

He and Donn shared a look. *It's happening. We've not stopped General Serras.*

"The General and Primus Ues ordered you detained. I cannot let you go."

Donn moved with such speed that the young man named Asof took an involuntary step backwards.

Donn was menacing, face to face with the Asof, now. "You know who I am, who he is? If you lift a finger against the Sunborn line, I will kill you. You think I need a sword? I was trained by the masters of the blade AND of the hand. I can kill you with three fingers, boy."

All Landorian princes spent time in the army, to learn, to watch, to absorb from leaders. It had been this way for generations. They held no power. No sway. Their fathers and mothers giving them up to learn.

To serve.

But Dragh held his breath, hoping that his name meant something to this young man.

Asof gulped some air, shook a little, but stood his ground. Puffing out his chest in fake confidence.

"Please," He said, his eyes begging Donn not to push it.

Dragh stepped around the young guard and gripped Donn's shoulder.

"Donn," Dragh calmed the Legate.

"Look Asof, we need to stop this. They are going to kill hundreds of women and children. People like your mother, your sister, your brothers. Your family. They are innocent in this. We cannot allow it. That is why we are stuck here. They are asking you to be party to *murder.*"

Asof sucked in a breath.

Dragh knew that most men had never questioned their orders, never asked why. But today, Asof was facing a choice. Was he going to do what was right, or what was ordered by the General himself?

Dragh could see the battle within the young man, a Sunborn's request in Landor and her provinces was an order. The young man was torn between following orders and following the request of the crown.

"Asof, the General is about to do something that will stain the Sunborn name for a generation. More. If we do not get out of here. If you do not let us out of here, there will be no one to stop it," Donn met Asof's gaze, moving his head to the side, putting his hands up in surrender to the boy.

Donn stepped forward. "Be brave Asof."

Asof's shoulders slumped. He looked down at his feet.

Dragh stepped between Donn and Asof. "It's okay. I'll make this right. I will protect you from this, you have my word as the Prince of Landor, as a Sunborn."

Asof looked back and forth again, the beading sweat on his brow falling, his face flush. "I cannot do that. The General ordered me to guard your tent. There are two more men out front."

Dragh nodded to Donn.

The Praetorian had edged his way to Asof's side.

The blow that put the young man into darkness was fast, practiced by the Praetorians and soldiers to incapacitate without killing.

Asof fell to the ground without a word, his only mark of understanding the betrayal in his eyes just before he dropped.

"We need to move. Now," Dragh said, readying himself for what was next.

Donn nodded to Dragh. "No sense in telling you we need to get to your father? That this is folly to try and stop an army that you have no command of?"

Dragh stood tall. "I'm a Sunborn. This is my army."

Donn smiled and nodded. "Fuckin' Serras,"

Dragh chuckled. "My thoughts exactly."

Donn moved ahead of Dragh, producing a small knife from inside his red and gold tunic, one the guards had missed when they frisked him.

Dragh did the same.

He'd learned from Donn, his tricks, his strategy. More than any General he'd followed in his time with the army.

Donn cut the fabric of the tent, from above his head to his feet, stopping before he cut through the whole sheet, to stop it from billowing in the wind.

Dragh followed the Praetorian out the back of the tent and into the camp's maze.

They walked, quickly, but didn't run.

Running drew the eye.

They acted like they belonged.

Dragh looked back and forth, scanning for trouble, listening to see if the two guards outside had discovered Asof.

Eventually they would.

They moved through the camp, between the tents, stopping to check each intersection.

"Here." Donn said, kneeling down beside a small tent, pulling back the door flap. "Clear."

Dragh stepped in behind Donn.

The tent was a double, smaller the Donn and Dragh's, with two bed rolls and two armour trees. A cross with leather padded armor and brass helmets on them.

Donn pulled the armor off one tree and handed it to Dragh. "Put it on, we cannot afford to be spotted."

Dragh pulled the leather armor over his tunic and then donned the helmet. The smell of sweat was sweet and sickly in the strangers armour.

Dragh felt excitement in his veins again.

And then, with the sharp shouts of thwarted men from behind him, among the white tents of the Landor Army, dread.

They were coming.

CHAPTER SIX

"How do we stop Serras?" Dragh looked at Donn as they crouched behind a white tent.

The clouds had moved in above them; darkness covered the camp, grey clouds bringing trouble rolled in underneath the sun.

"We've tried to stop him with words," Donn said, leaving the implication hanging between them.

"We can't kill a General. We need to try again, to rally my nobles to me. They will speak sense into Serras. The Legates cannot ignore that I am of the blood,"

Donn sighed. "You're right, young Sunborn, but if all else fails, what are you willing to do to stop this?"

Dragh paused for a moment. "He will listen, he will have to listen to reason Donn."

"Only a King can command a General. You know this. The Council ensured it after the Cleansing." Donn reminded Dragh, showing a moment of hesitancy.

All knew of the Cleansing, when the Council broke the last empire.

"It matters not Donn, I am a Sunborn. I must do what I can to protect these people. Baratan is my responsibility."

Donn nodded. "They will be taking Ues and a couple of Squads, like the General had commanded you to do, They will leave a skeleton force here to protect their rear.

"We take horses, ride out and tell the army that they have to stop."

Dragh felt anger at Serras, at Ues. They were forcing him to do something that his entire being rebelled against. His own mind protested his path. But Dragh knew what he had to do. He had to stop this killing.

Donn put his hand on Dragh's shoulder. "I will always be with you Dragh. Till the end."

Dragh pulled Donn in, hugging the surprised Praetorian.

"Go," he said to Donn, smiling at the older man.

He'd not face his father, or any man, with these deaths, this blood on his hands.

He'd kill Serras himself if he had to, to stop this.

—--

They raced the main thoroughfare of the camp, straight down the gauntlet.

"We ride to the front," Dragh said, his face whipped with wind.

Dragh could see the battle of the mind on Donn's face.

"Go hard to the front, I'll make sure you make it!" Donn shouted, just a horse length behind him.

They hadn't been able to find Ferras and Donn's mount, but they'd taken two unattended horses from a picket just outside the south end of camp. They threw saddles on the beasts, cinched their belly belts and vaulted into the saddle.

Dragh could see Baratan in the distance to the south now, straight ahead.

White tents and shouting men were on either side of them as they raced through camp.

Men of the Eighth were assembling due south, readying to assault the village of Baratan. The glint of spears, of helmets and shields polished to a shine was like a sea of stars on the plain between Dragh and Baratan. He could see the Legion's men arrayed for war, arrayed for killing in row upon row.

Two men, brave to a fault, threw themselves in front of Dragh and Donn.

Dragh could see at the last moment, one of them was the confused and stumbling Asof.

Dragh closed his eyes. They were too close to stop, too close to chance any outcome.

It didn't hurt any less. The thud of flesh on the front of his horse's chest was the only sound he heard.

Wet. Meaty.

Dragh opened his eyes, a tear rolling from his eyes that had nothing to do with the wind.

Moments later, they were through the camp. Through the rows and rows of white and into the open plain before Baratan.

The Eighth now stood between them and the village.

Dragh veered his horse to the right, still trying to find the gait of the unfamiliar beast.

It was time to stop General Serras.

Dragh clenched his jaw. He was about to test the bounds of his authority.

In hundreds of years, he'd never learned of a prince challenging a General he was in service to. Never learned of a circumstance where it was needed.

Would his ancestors, the Sunborns, have killed these people? Would his father have allowed it?

Doubt crept into his mind as he and Donn raced around the squads of the Eighth. Dragh knew that if he stopped this madness, he would be justified in his fight against the General. If he failed, his enemies would write his story. He would be painted as an enemy, an entitled prince who would not fall in line.

General Searras had aligned the squads, three deep, with the Cavalry and his commanders at the center of the front line. Dragh had once felt comfort in the formation, sitting atop his own horse within the Eight's squad of cavalry. Now, it was a threat to his life, to those of the people of Baratan's.

Dragh rounded the end on the west side, hugging the line. He was now between the Eighth and the village, racing inward.

None of the soldiers reacted, none shouted. They were two men on Landorian horses, with Landorian colors on.

Red and gold, the color of his line.

Dragh aimed at the center's flank; the cavalry was moving faster than the troops on foot.

Donn matched him, pulling up to ride neck in neck between him and the Eighth.

The Command was punched out, marching ahead of the Cavalry in the center of the force.

Shouts rose up in front of them from the Cavalry.

They knew Dragh, they knew Donn.

"GENERAL!" Dragh shouted, skidding to a halt, his mount digging its rear hooves in as Dragh yanked hard back on the rein.

"GENERAL SERRAS!" Dragh shouted, just horse lengths away from the General, his Legates and Primus'.

The General walked his horse out of the pack leading the Eighth to face Dragh.

"I'll give you one more chance to leave, Dragh. One more chance to regain your honor before I have you removed from the field."

The offer gave Dragh pause. Would the General really let him walk away after what he'd done? Could he live with himself if he did?

Dragh shook his head. "I give you one more chance, General. Stop this madness now. I command you as the Prince, Dragh Sunborn. Stand these men down. Stop this madness!"

General Serras scoffed and looked back at the Eighth before addressing Dragh. "You have no power here Prince."

"You think my father would stand for this to be done in his name? You're insane. I'll have you stripped of your title, your command. You'll be sharpening arrows in the Skellen Pass by the time I'm done with you," Dragh shot back.

General Serras lost composure for a moment.

Dragh pushed his horse forward, closer to the General. "Serras, I beg you, please stop this. Baratan and her people have paid the price for their insolence. A generation of their men are gone. It will take them decades to recover from what we've done. It is enough."

Dragh and Serras sharred a moment, meeting each others gaze. Dragh knew in that moment that he'd lost this fight. That the General had no intention of letting these people live.

"Get this stain off the battlefield!" Serras shouted, pointing at Dragh and Donn.

Seven horsemen moved forward from the ranks, dismounting their horses.

Dragh knew them all, not by name, but by face.

Except for one. Primus Ues.

"Stop this right now, in the name of the King!" Dragh shouted.

The men paused, looking uncertain, looking to each other.

Dragh and Donn both were dressed in red and gold. Dragh's family colors.

"He has no authority here! Listen to the General!" Ues shouted at the stopped men.

Donn pulled out his sword, brandishing the weapons they'd found with the saddles of the horses they'd stolen.

"Any of you threaten the Prince, you will all die." Donn pointed the sword at the men.

"You two, with me," Ues said to the men on his right. "You four, kill the traitor," He nodded to the men on his left, then to Donn.

"Stop this! I command you!" Dragh shouted, a last ditch effort.

Dragh looked around to the men of the Eigth. "Rikos! Wents! Garvel! Anyone! This is insanity. Stop this mindless killing. I will not have it!"

The Eighth stood still. None moved.

"Dragh. We are alone now. It is time."

Dragh felt the weight of his decision. The weight of what he'd asked of Donn.

They were going to die.

Three men, Ues included, moved on Dragh, four on Donn. They knew their opponents.

It would take all of them to contain one of the best killers in Landor. There was a reason his father had sent the Praetorian to protect Dragh.

"Blood and Honor!" Donn shouted as the four horsemen bore down on him.

Dragh saw the twin blades of Donn glinting, even in the pale light of the clouded day.

Dragh screamed no war cry, no words for the scum that came for him. He raised his sword, sending a prayer to the gods.

"Rikos! Wents! Garin! To me!" Dragh shouted into the Cavalry.

General Serras laughed.

"You think those boys will betray their General? They lack the spine," Ues sneered at Dragh and Donn.

Dragh caught Rikos's eye in the crowd of men seated on their horses. Shame painted his face and he looked away.

Dragh felt the betrayal of his friend cut into his heart. He ached from it.

He'd been sure they'd side with him. Sure that they'd choose the side of right.

"You've lost, boy. Now get out of my way, before I have you put down."

A loud whistle, then another, and another began behind them, from the troops that had stopped.

Dragh paused. The three men facing him, Primus Ues in the center, did as well.

Dragh grinned at them.

Arrows rained down on the men facing Dragh and Donn, streaking through the air, the whistle of death on their fletching.

Dragh watched the first arrow bury itself to the fletching in the man to Ues' right. The fletching was red, the color of the roosters that the bowyers used in Landor.

"SUNBORN, I AM WITH YOU!" Harvel shouted. The archer ran from the ranks of the Eighth behind the cavalry squads.

For a moment Dragh was shocked. His Nobles, the men he'd rode with as a boy. The men that he'd learned with in the army, had abandoned him. The lone archer, a man from among the common folk of Landor, had chosen him.

He would not waste Harvel's efforts.

Dragh launched himself forward as the soldiers of the Eighth looked up at the missiles from Harvel raining down of them.

Arrows fell around Ues and the other cavalry man. Dragh put his faith in the gods that he wouldn't be hit. Dragh almost laughed, when it was his enemy it was cowardice, but now, feeling the protection of his own archer, he felt invulnerable to the missiles from up above.

The first man came abreast Ues, Dragh struck out with his boot, feeling the contact with the soldiers chest. The rush of air as he expelled his breath audible.

Dragh blocked Ues strike from the side, the jarring blow vibrating his sword arm and shoulder. The wound from the chase the day before aching.

Dragh spun his horse, pushing the second solider away from him, trying to create space to fight each man, one on one. He pushed his sword up, catching Ues in the air above their heads. He head putted Ues, sending the man back, reeling in his saddle.

One cavalry man was on the ground, dead.

Dragh knew then that he'd need to save Donn.

"Finally showing your true colors Sunborn!" Ues reeled back and spit blood.

Dragh wiped at his eyes, blinking hard to clear them both. He glanced over to Donn, who was now on foot. His horse dead beside him.

Twin blades flashed at the Cavalry men who circled him.

Striking out at Ues, he gave himself distance to push towards Donn, to his right.

"Yah!" Dragh kicked his horse into action, trying to get to Donn, to help him.

The cavalry man who'd stepped in with Ues to help contain Dragh was mid-shout when an arrow pierced his head, through the skull, exiting his face.

A gift from Harvel.

Turning to Donn again, Dragh pushed forward.

Dragh watched as one of the men was skewered by one Donn's sword, the blade entering his stomach and exiting his back.

At the same time, another of the enemy thrust forward. Donn blocked the first blow, but couldn't pull his other blade free. The enemy parried Donn's second block, rolling his blade, plunging it into Donn's chest.

"NOO!" Dragh screamed.

Donn looked down, releasing his swords and grabbing the blade by its naked edge.

Donn pulled the rider forward by his blade, drew his dagger and stabbed the man in the eye socket.

The man dropped, and after a moment, so did Donn.

"DONN!" Dragh screamed, hacking and slashing as he felt hot tears on his face.

Horsemen whirled around the fallen man, some trampling on the fallen Praetorian, some just kicking up dust.

Dragh dove forward onto the ground, towards Donn.

Donn looked up at Dragh, a bloody smile on his face.

"DONN!" Dragh shouted again. He felt something inside of him tearing, wrenching free, like the snapping of a tree branch.

Hot tears spilled down his face.

Dragh felt cold seep into his heart. Knowing that getting to the Praetorian wasn't enough, knowing that Donn was going to die.

He hacked and slashed at the men around Donn, trying desperately to change what was happening.

Dragh never saw the blow that unhorsed him. A blow from behind, sharp. He saw stars as he tumbled, losing his grip on his own sword.

Dragh coughed as he breathed in dust, his lungs not able to get enough oxygen.

He tried to blink it out, but he was suddenly surrounded by boots.

Try as he might, Dragh couldn't help but scream out in pain. Feet kicking him connected with his face, his torso, his ears.

Darkness closed in on him, his vision blurring.

The last person he saw was Donn, through the feet, through the dust that kicked up. His open dark eyes, unblinking in death.

CHAPTER SEVEN

"Up, you shite!"

Dragh rubbed at his eyes, his face sore from the beating he'd taken. A lump had risen on the back of his head from the blow that had knocked him unconscious on the battlefield.

Dragh pushed himself up, his face peeling off the granite floor he'd awoken on. He looked around for the voice, pushing to his feet.

Confused, he could see a shelf the size of a man that was cut into the granite, the floor and ceiling the same stone. A small lone window let feeble moonlight into the place.

"Get up and take your food, boy," The voice said again.

Dragh found the man's face in the darkness. A torch burned beside the man, light showing a round pudgy face with jiggling jowls. The man wore rags for clothes, but had a gold earring in his right ear.

"You soldiers are all the same, pompous. Do you want to eat? Well then, get over here before Barren spills it on the floor and you have a lick it off." The man laughed, wiggling a cup back and forth from beyond the bars in front of Dragh.

Bars separated the two of them.

Dragh walked to the man, and with horror realized that it was he that was behind bars.

The bars ran from the granite ceiling to the floor and crossed over each other, forming a wall of metal that was meant to keep Dragh in.

"Where—" Dragh coughed from his dry throat. "Where am I?"

Barren shook the cup, chunks of grey meat and thick juices spilling down the sides onto the floor. "Prison, you fool."

Dragh took the cup, his hand slipping.

"Ahhh, you almost went hungry," Barren said, turning to leave.

"Wait! Where am I?" Dragh pleaded, grabbing the bars of the cell.

Barren turned, whistling to himself. "They scrambled your eggs, huh?"

Dragh waited, his breath heavy, his heart pounding in his ears.

Barren gave a wicked smile. "You killed a man, one of your own. Landor Prison is your new home, *boy.*"

The jailer turned and walked away into the darkness; his whistling half-laugh echoing on the granite walls around him.

Dragh felt his heart stop, his breath catch.

He'd killed one of his own.

—--

The days and weeks blended. His only account of passing time the sun and moon, and Barren's daily visits.

Dragh's mind began to slip.

How could his father leave him here?

Why hadn''t he been released?

Does Barren know who he is?

Day after day, Dragh thought on his life.

What happened in Baratan? Did the Eighth kill them all? Did Dragh stop anything?

The prison gave him a meal a day. Some days Barren spilled it, some days he gave it to Dragh.

Even during the day, such a small amount of light came through the window up high that he was forever in semidarkness.

Barren didn't keep the torch lit.

"Waste of oil," he'd told Dragh on his second day there.

Dragh sat during the day, paced and then slept. No one to talk to but Barren, and himself.

I deserve this. I deserve to die here.

——

A new sound came down the hallway of granite. The echoing of steps sharper than Barren's padding in the stone hallway.

Dragh sat up on the cold hard granite slab he slept on.

"Where are you?" A voice cut through the dark.

Dragh felt his pulse quicken. "Uncle?" He dared not hope.

His Uncle Nestor appeared from the darkness, the shape of his face a mirage in the Pit that Dragh was in.

Dragh sat still, cursing himself. "Not even my father would sully himself with me now, huh?"

Nestor smiled in the darkness. "I'm here, boy."

Dragh kicked at the ground, rising and walking to the bars of the cell. "Harvel, is he alive?"

Nestor shook his head.

Dragh let the tears slip down his face. "Why am I still here Nestor?"

Nestor rubbed his face with one hand. "Aye my boy, you killed your own Primus. What did you expect, your father to back you?"

A silence stretched out between them. Uncle and nephew. An understanding of what the crown had done. What the crown had killed between father and son.

"I didn't know."

Nestor nodded. "You gutted him, his inside spilled out over his horse."

Dragh sat down on the granite bench in his cell, his head in his hands again. The world spun. He had killed Ues. A man of the Landorian Army.

"Donn? Baratan?" He asked, holding out hope that what he saw wasn't as bad as he thought.

The sharp blade piercing Donn's guts, four men against one.

Donn's blade had sung through the air. It's edge mastered by a swordsmen unapparelled in Landor.

"My men tell me he was killed by four. They tell me he took three with him."

Dragh wanted to scream, to kill Serras. To kill anyone involved.

Donn had helped raise him up. Helped him stay alive more times that he could count.

"They rolled over Baratan like a rogue wave over land. Swept it from the map. They claim that there were enemies of the crown harbored inside of Baratan. That their intelligence led them to attack the place.

Dragh paced the cell, the granite stone walls closing in on him. His head aching. All that innocent blood was on his hands. He'd failed.

He stopped in front of Nestor again. 'Serras?"

Nestor gave Dragh a sad look, pursing his lips.

Dragh felt empty. His stomach felt like it was dropping though his bowels.

"He backed Serras."

Dragh hung his head. His father had not come. He was still here. He would be here forever. For the unity of the crown and the army.

"He signed their death warrant, innocents, Nestor."

Nestor nodded.

"How could he do this?"

"Come join the Second. Don't waste your life away in here. I'll take you, train you, the right way. We Don't kill innocents, Dragh."

"I cannot," Dragh said, tears welling the corner of his eyes.

"You can still be King when this is over. Your father may have taken Serras' side, but he will soften in years to come. You will prove yourself in the Second."

Dragh laughed without humor.

"I have no father. I am no prince."

Nestor scoffed at that. "Your blood is up. In a year's time you will feel different."

Dragh turned away from Nestor, the hope that he'd felt in his stomach quickly crushed down by the guilt.

He killed his own. Even if the man was a shit heel. He had tried and failed to save Baratan. The people of the place. He'd failed to stop a massacre, his friends, his mentor, all dead now. His father and mother had abandoned him. Worse, his father had condoned the killing of innocents.

"Leave me," Dragh croaked, staring at the wall.

Nestor stayed there for moments, waiting.

Dragh closed his eyes and leaned his head on the wall.

"Don't do this, boy."

Dragh said nothing.

A sharp scraping noise told Dragh that Nestor had left. His footsteps echoing down the hall. The screaming of metal hinges and the clattering of the metal keeper closed Dragh into solitude again.

Darkness swallowed him, crushing him.

Dragh felt the reality of what he'd just done weigh down on him.

He'd be here until he died.

"Wait!" Dragh shouted, opening his eyes and turning back to the bars.

He lunged to the bars, closing the distance in one step across the cell.

"Uncle! Wait!'

Dragh waited, breathing hard. He couldn't see Nestor, only the depth of the stone hallway, and then nothing.

It was Dragh, alone, and the beating of his heart threatening to overwhelm his mind.

Thud, thud, thud, thud.

"NESTOR!" Dragh shouted, falling to the ground.

Tears fell from his face as he felt the truth settle over him. He didn't want to wear a crown any longer. He was a Sunborn, yes. But his family had betrayed him. His father his mother. He wanted more. He wanted to do what was right.

He would prove themn all wrong.

Thud, thud, thud, thud.

"Boy."

Dragh's head shot up.

"You've come to your senses?" Nestor lifted an eyebrow.

Dragh fixed his Uncle with a look through watery eyes. "I will join the Legion of Criminals Uncle. You'll have your prize. If the Sunborn crown is dipped in the blood of innocents, if it takes selling your soul, I will have no part in it."

Nestor stiffened at the proclamation. "You will forsake your father, your mother to join me in the Second?"

"Send me to the Pit, to the Car Lauch," Dragh said, letting out a raged breath. He felt tears welling in his eyes.

The mountains were where recruits of the Second were sent to become soldiers. Where the criminals learned to be real killers. The thought of the place gave Dragh the chills. He winced at the thought of what he was asking for.

"You need not go there. You're a soldier already. That is where we break men, Dragh, to make them into the Second." Nestor shook his head.

"I need to be one of them. I don't want them to know I'm a Sunborn," Dragh said.

Nestor looked over Dragh from head to toe. "You smell like you're from the streets, and by the look of that beard, you could pass for a rat."

Dragh snorted. "I will be one of your killers. My hands are already stained with blood,"

"Come with me then, boy. We'll show my brother Kallen what real men are made of."

Nestor shoved his hand through the bars of the cell.

Dragh looked at his uncle's hand for a moment and then pushed himself up. He gripped it in the soldier's way.

"Blood and Honor," Nestor said.

Dragh nodded. "Blood and Honor."

ACKNOWLEDGEMENTS

First to my wife and daughter. As always, your support, your kind words and your patience with my wild writers brain is a gift that I will always cherish. A million thank yous and all of my love. To Joan, for all of your thoughtful and kind feedback.

To my Beta readers, Josh, Rob, Wendy, thank you for all of your feedback. It takes a village to write a story. Thank you for being there for me.

To my editor Nathan Hall, thank you for your help in polishing the stone once again. I appreciate the sage advice.

To The Break Ins. In no particular order: Josh, Scott, Kaden, Calum, Adrian, Rob, Louise, Sam, Bryan, Andrew, Nick, Jonathan, Nicholas, Zac and Francisca. Thank you for the support, it's been a wild year of releases!

To my readers, I hope you enjoy the first Novella in the Sunborn Series! It's been an amazing journey with The Dragon Legion. Thank you for the support.

If you'd like to follow along, please sign up for my newsletter at www.isaachillauthor.com or follow me on Instagram / Twitter/ X: @isaachillauthor

HIC SUNT DRACONES!

ABOUT THE AUTHOR

I saac Hill is a self published fantasy and fiction Author from Nova Scotia, Canada. Isaac's current project is his Sunborn Series, a generational story of the Sunborn Empire. Isaac enjoys spending time with his wife and daughter in the great outdoors, reading a wide variety of stories and scribbling his own thoughts down in his spare time.

Isaac's hobbies are wide and varied. He's built boats, made his own traditional bows and raced on downhill skiing. Now, he collects books, typewriters and tells stories of his own. Inspired by David Gemmell, Pierce Brown and Anthony Ryan he tells stories of heroes, of deeds echoing through generations.